1812

CHANGES FOR
Caroline

BY KATHLEEN ERNST

ILLUSTRATIONS ROBERT PAPP

VIGNETTES LISA PAPP

★ American Girl®

THE AMERICAN GIRLS

KAYA, an adventurous Nez Perce girl whose deep love for horses and respect for nature nourish her spirit

1774

FELICITY, a spunky, spritely colonial girl, full of energy and independence

1812

CAROLINE, a daring, self-reliant girl who learns to steer a steady course amid the challenges of war

1824

JOSEFINA, a Hispanic girl whose heart and hopes are as big as the New Mexico sky

1853

CÉCILE AND MARIE-GRACE, two girls whose friendship helps them—and New Orleans— survive terrible times

1854

KIRSTEN, a pioneer girl of strength and spirit who settles on the frontier

1864  ADDY, a courageous girl determined to be free in the midst of the Civil War

1904  SAMANTHA, a bright Victorian beauty, an orphan raised by her wealthy grandmother

1914  REBECCA, a lively girl with dramatic flair growing up in New York City

1934  KIT, a clever, resourceful girl facing the Great Depression with spirit and determination

1944  MOLLY, who schemes and dreams on the home front during World War Two

1974  JULIE, a fun-loving girl from San Francisco who faces big changes—and creates a few of her own

Questions or comments? Call 1-800-845-0005, visit **americangirl.com**,
or write to Customer Service, American Girl, 8400 Fairway Place,
Middleton, WI 53562-0497.

Printed in China
13 14 15 16 17 18 19 20 LEO 10 9 8 7 6 5 4 3 2

Deep appreciation to Constance Barone, Director, Sackets Harbor Battlefield
State Historic Site; Dianne Graves, historian; James Spurr, historian and First Officer,
Friends Good Will, Michigan Maritime Museum; and Stephen Wallace, former Interpretive
Programs Assistant, Sackets Harbor Battlefield State Historic Site.

PICTURE CREDITS
The following individuals and organizations have generously given permission
to reprint images contained in "Looking Back": p. 77—North Wind Picture Archives;
pp. 78–79—Amedée Forestier, Library and Archives Canada, C-115678 (diplomats in Ghent);
William L. Clements Library, University of Michigan (treaty signatures); Library of Congress,
Prints and Photographs Division, LC-DIG-pga-01838 (Battle of New Orleans); North Wind Picture
Archives (celebration); pp. 80–81—Old Sturbridge Village Collections, Sturbridge, MA (factory);
courtesy of U.S. Naval Academy Museum (naval battle); North Wind Picture Archives (covered
wagon, field being cleared); pp. 82–83—Genesee Country Village and Museum (cabin);
North Wind Picture Archives (girl milking cow); © Bettmann/Corbis (Erie Canal);
pp. 84–85—© iStockphoto/Alija (Statue of Liberty); © Tom Grill/Corbis (farmland);
© iStockphoto/ekash (Golden Gate Bridge).

Library of Congress Control Number: 2012947791

FOR MY FRIENDS AT AMERICAN GIRL,
PAST AND PRESENT, WHO HAVE HELPED
MAKE EACH BOOK THE BEST IT CAN BE

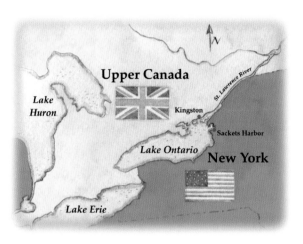

Caroline Abbott is growing up in Sackets Harbor, New York, right on the shore of Lake Ontario. Just across the lake is the British colony of *Upper Canada*.

In 1812, the nation of Canada didn't exist yet. Instead, the lands north of the Great Lakes were still a collection of British colonies. Today, Upper Canada is the Canadian province of Ontario.

In Caroline's time, there was a colony called *Lower Canada,* too. It stretched from Upper Canada eastward to the Atlantic Ocean. Today, it's the province of Quebec.

TABLE OF CONTENTS

CAROLINE'S FAMILY AND FRIENDS

CAROLINE'S FAMILY

PAPA
Caroline's father, a fine shipbuilder who owns Abbott's Shipyard

MAMA
Caroline's mother, a firm but understanding woman

CAROLINE
A daring girl who wants to be captain of her own ship one day

GRANDMOTHER
Mama's widowed mother, who makes her home with the Abbott family

LYDIA
Caroline's twelve-year-old cousin and good friend, who is helping on her parents' new farm

**UNCLE AARON &
AUNT MARTHA**
*Caroline's uncle and aunt,
who have moved to
a farm in New York*

MR. TATE
*The chief carpenter at
Abbott's and a friend
of Caroline's family*

CHAPTER
ONE

UNCLE AARON'S
LETTER

Merow!

"Hush, Inkpot," Caroline murmured.

She'd been dreaming about sailing Lake Ontario with Papa. A breeze kept them flying over the waves. Sunshine glistened on the water. Caroline didn't want to wake up.

The cat pawed her cheek. *Merow!*

Caroline sat up in bed, rubbing her eyes. Inkpot clearly had important business elsewhere. Caroline didn't know how long she'd been asleep, but the room was dark. She scooped the cat into her arms.

"Do you need to go outside?" Caroline whispered. Inkpot nudged her chin. *I'd better take you downstairs,* she thought. She didn't want the cat to wake anyone.

The June night was pleasant, warm but not hot. Caroline padded silently down the steps. Her eyes were adjusting to the darkness, so she had no trouble making her way to the front door.

"Catch lots of mice!" she whispered. When she cracked the door open, Inkpot bounded into the night.

As Caroline turned back, she noticed a faint glow coming from the parlor. She peeked inside. Papa sat at the writing table in the far corner, studying some papers by the light of a single candle.

"Papa?" she called softly.

He blinked and looked up, clearly startled. Then he smiled. "Caroline! What are you doing up at this hour?" He held out one hand with a look that said, *Please, come join me.*

Caroline pattered across the floor and leaned against him. "Inkpot wanted to go outside," she explained. "What are *you* doing up?"

"I couldn't sleep," he told her. "So I . . ." He gestured toward the papers.

Caroline saw that he'd been sketching a sloop. "Oh, Papa! It's a *beautiful* ship." Her father was a shipbuilder—the best in all of New York, as far as she was concerned.

"I had many ideas for new designs while I was a prisoner," Papa said, "but no paper or pencil."

Caroline nodded. When America declared war on Great Britain a year ago, Papa had been captured and held as a prisoner in Upper Canada. He'd managed to escape and make the dangerous journey back to Sackets Harbor. Having him home these past weeks had been wonderful! After missing Papa for so many months, Caroline didn't think she would *ever* catch up on time spent with him.

She took a closer look at the sketches. Abbott's Shipyard was making gunboats for the American navy now, but Caroline was glad to see that Papa was still thinking about the pretty merchant ships he loved to design. The British had stolen the last sloop her father had built, a sweet ship called *White Gull*. And she had destroyed her father's little skiff earlier that spring, sinking it to block a creek and keep a British warship from capturing American supplies. Without the skiff, she and Papa couldn't take even short trips on the water. "Oh, Papa," she said

with a big sigh, "I wish we still had *Sparrow*. I do sorely miss sailing with you out on the lake!"

Papa squeezed her shoulder. "I miss that as well, daughter," he said. "One day we'll be able to sail clear across Lake Ontario again whenever we wish."

Caroline watched a moth flutter near the candle, then dance away. "I hope so," she said. "Sometimes it feels as if this war will never end."

"Don't lose faith." Papa's voice was low but firm. "Soon we'll celebrate Independence Day. That will remind us that America has not been defeated!"

The reminder of Independence Day pushed away Caroline's gloomy thoughts. "I *am* excited about the celebration," she told him, bouncing on her toes. "Surely everyone in Sackets Harbor will gather! I've heard there will be music and speeches and a gun salute—even a concert by the navy musicians."

Papa smiled and then turned back to his drawing. Caroline felt very special, alone here with Papa while the rest of the house slept. It was a delicious treat to share this quiet time with him. She rested her head against his shoulder and studied his new design. With just a few pencil strokes, Papa had captured the sloop's graceful lines.

It was a delicious treat to share this quiet time with Papa.
Caroline rested her head against his shoulder and studied his new design.

5

Caroline let her imagination wander back to the last time they'd sailed the lake together. She could almost hear timbers creaking and sails snapping in the wind. She could almost smell the fresh paint and damp breeze. She could almost feel the deck rocking gently beneath her feet. Her heart squeezed with longing to be back out on the water.

"Papa," Caroline whispered, "do you think you might one day build a sloop for me?" She held her breath.

Papa was silent. Caroline wondered if he was remembering the last time she'd asked that question—right before they learned that their country was at war. "You're too flighty, Caroline," he'd told her that day. And, "If you want to sail on the Great Lakes, you must stay *steady*."

Now she added, "I've tried to be steady, Papa. I've tried to help Mama and Grandmother, and help at the shipyard, and . . ." Her voice trailed away. The last year had been so hard! She had made some mistakes, but she had also tried to prove to her family and friends that they could depend on her.

Papa touched her cheek. "My little Caroline," he said softly. "You're becoming such a fine young lady."

Caroline felt her hopes slide back toward her bare toes. *Fine young lady?* That was a nice compliment, but what she *wanted* to hear was Papa's assurance that he'd seen how steady and responsible she'd become while he was away.

Papa pulled her around to stand before his chair so that he could look at her directly. "It's very late, daughter." He leaned forward and kissed her forehead. "Go back to bed."

*I don't **want** to go back to bed*, Caroline thought. "But—" she began, before cutting the protest short. "Yes, Papa." She gave him a quick hug and left him alone with his own thoughts and dreams.

When Caroline woke, sun was streaming through the window. The scent of frying bacon drifted into the bedroom. She tossed the quilt aside and jumped to her feet. If she didn't hurry, she'd be late for breakfast.

A few moments later, Caroline skidded into the kitchen. She was glad to see her parents still at the table with Grandmother. Mama and Papa both worked at the shipyard now, and they often left home early.

"Gracious," Mama said. "Such a clatter!"

Grandmother added, "I thought that was a horse galloping down the stairs, not a young lady." Her eyes were merry, though. Caroline suspected that when Grandmother was a girl, she'd galloped down stairs sometimes, too.

Caroline swallowed a laugh before dutifully saying, "I'm sorry." She took her place at the table. "May I go to the shipyard today?"

"It's baking day, Caroline," Grandmother reminded her.

"I meant, may I go to the shipyard after chores," Caroline said quickly. Baking was one of her least favorite activities, and usually their boarder, Mrs. Hathaway, helped Grandmother. Mrs. Hathaway had taken her daughters to visit relatives in Albany, however. Caroline knew she had to pitch in.

She was reaching for the milk jug when someone knocked on the front door.

"I'll get it," Mama said. She rose and wiped her hands on her apron before hurrying from the room. Caroline heard the murmur of voices in the hall.

A moment later Mama returned, holding a folded piece of paper.

"What is it?" Papa asked.

"A letter from my brother Aaron," Mama replied. "His neighbor, Mr. Sinclair, brought it."

"Oh, good!" Caroline said. "I've been waiting to hear how Lydia likes the new farm." Caroline's cousin Lydia, Aunt Martha, and Uncle Aaron had fled Upper Canada the previous autumn, leaving behind their farm, their oxen and chickens and pigs, and many of their tools and household belongings. Uncle Aaron had recently purchased a farm several miles from Sackets Harbor. Caroline hadn't seen Lydia since she and her parents had moved to their new home.

Mama broke the circle of hardened wax that sealed the letter and began to read aloud.

My dear sister,

We recently received word that Martha's eldest sister is gravely ill. Martha packed a few things and left at once to tend to her.

As you know, starting a new farm here in New York has taken every penny we had. We

*used the last of our cash to buy a cow and her calf.
Lydia is struggling to manage both the house and
the cows while I work the fields.*

"Oh, poor Lydia," Caroline said. She could well
imagine how hard Lydia must be working.

*The success of our new farm depends on
making a good start this summer. We must have
a good harvest if we are to have any hope of
surviving next winter. Therefore, I ask that you
send Caroline to us right away. We will likely
need her for some time to come.*

Caroline gasped. She was to go to the farm?
Right away? Without knowing when she might
return? A band seemed to go tight around her chest.
Mama pressed her lips together, as if she were
struggling too. Finally she finished reading the letter.

*I write in haste, as my neighbors, Mr. and
Mrs. Sinclair, are eager to leave for Sackets
Harbor. They have promised to deliver this letter
to you. Their business in the village will take an*

hour or so, no more. When they are finished, they
will call upon you again and escort Caroline to the
farm. May God keep you all.

Your brother,
Aaron Livingston

Caroline finally found her voice. "An hour?
So *soon?*" The last word came out as a squeak.

Mama and Papa shared a silent look. Then Mama
slid next to Caroline and pulled her close. "Surely
you will not hesitate," she said. "Lydia would help us
if the situation were reversed."

"I want to help," Caroline said. "It's just that . . ."
She looked at her father.

"We'll miss you very much," Papa told her. "But
I know you will be a great help on the farm."

Caroline struggled to find words. This was
happening so fast! Papa had been home for only a
few weeks. Now she was about to be taken away from
him, and Mama, and Grandmother. And Inkpot.

Away from the lake, too, Caroline thought. Her
cousin's new farm was well inland, miles away from
the lakeshore. Far away from her dream of once again
sailing over Lake Ontario's dancing waves.

Well, one thing was certain—complaining wouldn't help anything.

Caroline stood. "Excuse me," she said quietly. "I'd best go upstairs and pack."

MEETING GARNET

All too soon, the Sinclairs' farm wagon carried Caroline into the forest beyond Sackets Harbor. She answered questions politely, trying to pretend that she felt cheerful about the trip.

Finally Mrs. Sinclair asked kindly, "Are you getting tired, Caroline?"

"A little," Caroline admitted. She'd been clutching the wagon seat as they bucked and jounced over the rough road. Her hands ached, and she felt rattled all the way to her bones. *Traveling by water is so much nicer than traveling on land*, she thought.

Mr. Sinclair gave her an encouraging smile. "We're getting close to your uncle's farm."

Caroline's heart grew heavier with every moment that the horse plodded away from her family, away from Lake Ontario, away from *home*. She knew that Mr. and Mrs. Sinclair were doing Uncle Aaron a favor by bringing her, though, and she didn't want to seem ungrateful. "It was kind of you to fetch me," she said.

"It was no trouble," Mrs. Sinclair assured her. "Everyone in these parts is neighborly, always glad to help someone out."

"Well, not everybody," Mr. Sinclair muttered.

Caroline frowned. Was Mr. Sinclair thinking about someone in particular?

Mrs. Sinclair patted Caroline's knee. "Our neighbors are good people, but we seem to have a troublemaker skulking about. One of my best laying hens disappeared from my coop last week. Our closest neighbor had rhubarb cut right out of her garden."

"It's this war." Mr. Sinclair sounded disgusted. "The thief might be a deserter who ran off from the army or navy and is hiding in the woods. Or perhaps a soldier is sneaking away from camp, looking for fresh food."

"We've had trouble like that in Sackets Harbor,

too," Caroline told them. "The soldiers and sailors get tired of eating dried peas and salt pork, so they raid people's gardens." She had no sympathy for thieves. No matter how boring the soldiers' meals were, stealing was wrong!

"Let's talk of more pleasant things," Mrs. Sinclair said. "Caroline, Mr. Sinclair and I are having a picnic on Independence Day. You'll be able to meet everyone who lives in these parts."

"That sounds nice." Caroline tried to smile, but the news didn't lift her spirits. She wanted to be with her family on Independence Day! She turned her head so the Sinclairs wouldn't see that she was already homesick.

The passing view only reminded Caroline that she was traveling farther and farther from home. Instead of a bustling village, she saw only a few scattered farms in the woods. Instead of smelling Lake Ontario's damp tang, she inhaled the scent of road dust. Instead of feeling a cool breeze blowing in from open water, her skin prickled with sweat.

When the wagon passed little clearings in the forest, Caroline glimpsed people hanging laundry or hoeing weeds or chopping firewood. The settlers seemed isolated from their neighbors. *It would be easy for a thief to watch one of these little farms from the woods,* she thought, *just waiting for the chance to snatch something for his supper.* Caroline rubbed her arms, feeling chilled. Had thieves troubled Uncle Aaron and Lydia?

"Here we are," Mr. Sinclair said. He turned the horse into a narrow lane that led to a farmyard. "Whoa now, Bess."

Finally! Caroline gratefully unclenched her fingers from the seat.

Lydia ran from the cabin to meet the wagon. "Caroline!" she cried.

Caroline scrambled to the ground and hugged her cousin. "I've come to help."

"I'm *so* glad." Lydia stepped back and gestured widely with one arm. "Welcome to our farm."

Caroline looked around. The farm looked . . . well, ragged. The clearing was stubbled with rocks. The only buildings were a small log cabin and an animal shed. Corn and pumpkins grew in straggly patches in a field still full of stumps. Potatoes had been planted in fence corners. Caroline tried to hide her dismay. No wonder Uncle Aaron had sent for her! Any help she gave Lydia with gardening and household chores would let her uncle spend more time in the field.

"Papa was able to buy this farm for a low price because the previous owners cleared very little land before they moved on again," Lydia said. "I know it doesn't look like much—"

"But it will soon," Caroline said firmly.

Uncle Aaron hurried across the yard. "Thank you for coming, Caroline," he said. "Is your family well?"

"Yes," she told him. "They all send greetings."

Uncle Aaron thanked Mr. and Mrs. Sinclair for bringing Caroline. "I'll be by your place on Thursday to help cut your hay," he promised. He handed Mrs. Sinclair a little crock. "Here's some fresh butter—a gift from Minerva."

Caroline leaned close to Lydia and whispered, "Who is Minerva?"

Lydia waved good-bye to her neighbors before answering. "Our cow! Would you like to see her and the calf?"

"I would," Caroline told her.

Lydia led the way into the animal shed, where

a cow stood in a square stall. "Oh, my!" Caroline gasped. She had sometimes seen whole herds of cows being driven through Sackets Harbor, but she'd never been so close to a cow before. Here inside this little shed, Minerva looked very big! She was reddish-brown—except for her long, curved horns, which were cream-colored. *I will have to stay away from those horns,* Caroline thought.

Then the calf appeared from behind Minerva, walking on knobby legs. The calf was the same color as her mother. She had black eyes and long eyelashes. Caroline felt her heart melt like butter in the sun. "Oh, she's sweet," Caroline said. "What's her name?"

"She doesn't have one yet," Lydia told her. "Papa and I decided to let you name her."

"Truly?" Caroline asked. What an honor! She studied the calf thoughtfully. "Do you remember Grandmother's garnet ring—the one Grandfather gave her when they were courting? The calf is as red as the garnet stone. Let's call her that."

"I like that," Lydia said. "Garnet it shall be."

Caroline leaned over the stall railing. The little

calf had captured her heart. "I think you and I are going to be friends," Caroline whispered to the calf. "Good friends indeed."

That afternoon Caroline helped Lydia heat water and scrub milk pans, buckets, and a butter churn. "Having a dairy cow is a lot of work," Lydia told her. "When we finish washing these things, we'll put them away in the springhouse."

"Where is the springhouse?" Caroline asked.

Lydia handed her two tin milk pans to carry. "Come along. I'll show you."

The springhouse was built into the side of a hill in the woods behind the cowshed. It was so overgrown with blackberry brambles that Caroline barely saw the door before Lydia opened it. The springhouse was dim inside and smelled like damp earth. A shallow stream ran right through one corner, keeping the room cool. "This is like a hidden cave!" Caroline marveled as her eyes adjusted to the gloom.

"The springhouse was here when we bought the

farm," Lydia said. "It's bigger than we need right now."

"Well," Caroline said, "perhaps one day you'll have a whole herd of cows."

"I like that idea." Lydia grinned. "It would keep me busy, though. See those wooden racks?" She pointed to one wall. "After I milk Minerva, I pour the fresh milk into these pans and put them on the racks to cool. When the cream rises to the top, I skim it off and save it until I have enough to churn into butter."

"Doesn't Garnet need all of Minerva's milk?" Caroline asked.

"I'm milking Minerva only once a day, so there's plenty left for Garnet," Lydia explained. "Besides, Minerva sometimes pushes Garnet away now. She knows her calf is old enough to start eating on her own. You and I must coax Garnet along, because I really need all of Minerva's milk! I can sell butter at the general store, or trade it for other supplies."

Caroline nodded. She'd never thought about how precious milk or butter could be.

"Sometimes I daydream about buying sugar and baking something sweet," Lydia said. "We haven't had a bit of sugar since we came here." Then she folded her arms, looking determined. "That's no matter, really. What *is* important is growing enough food this summer to last us through the winter. We're not eating much now but dried peas and beans. I'm so hungry for something different!"

I should have brought food with me, Caroline thought. At home, there were still dried apples and turnips and sweet potatoes in her family's root cellar, and more were available in the market stalls near the harbor. She hadn't realized how hard it would be to find food on a new farm in early summer, when harvesttime for most crops was still many months away.

That evening the girls made a kettle of bean soup for supper. "You can see why we need your help," Uncle Aaron told Caroline as they settled at the table. "I need to work in the field, and Lydia can't manage Minerva, the garden, cooking, and household chores by herself. Caroline, I know you'll be a big help with chores. Will you also take charge of teaching Garnet to eat on her own? I'd like you to get her used to being led, too."

"I'm happy to!" Caroline assured him as she scooped up a spoonful of soup. Other than Inkpot, she'd never had the chance to take care of a baby animal before.

"We need your help with something else, too," Uncle Aaron said with a sigh. "Lately some of our neighbors have had eggs stolen from their chicken coops, and vegetables taken right from their gardens."

"The Sinclairs told me about that," Caroline said.

Lydia looked worried. "Yesterday I left a pail of milk sitting near the shed by mistake," she said. "When I went to fetch it later, the pail was gone."

Uncle Aaron leaned his forearms on the table and looked at Caroline. "We all must keep watch for anyone sneaking about our property. If you see anyone, fetch me at once."

"I will," Caroline promised. She hoped the thief would stay far away from their farm.

Uncle Aaron and Lydia were quiet. *They have more challenges than I even imagined,* Caroline thought. She looked around the little cabin—just one room and a loft. She and her parents had once lived in a log cabin, but she remembered it as a cheerful place, with pretty embroidered samplers on the wall and colorful woven coverlets on the beds. The Livingstons hadn't been able to take such treasures with them when they fled from Upper Canada. This cabin looked bare and lonely.

Caroline turned to her cousin. "Lydia, I brought some sewing supplies. Perhaps we can start making a quilt."

Lydia's face broke into a grateful smile. "Oh, I'd like that!"

That night, Caroline and Lydia settled down in the loft. Lydia fell asleep quickly, and Caroline soon heard her uncle snoring downstairs. She eased from the bed and tiptoed to the window. Nothing moved in the clearing below. The stumps in the field looked like strange, hunched creatures in the moonlight. She tried to get her bearings so that she could look toward Lake Ontario. Toward home. *I want to help Lydia and Uncle Aaron,* she thought. *But I wish their farm wasn't so far from Sackets Harbor.* Now, with everything silent and no chores or conversation to fill her hands and her mind, homesickness rushed back.

The best thing I can do is keep busy, Caroline reminded herself. That wouldn't be hard! Not with dairy chores, gardening, cooking, cleaning, sewing, and especially tending Minerva and Garnet.

Caroline nodded, feeling determined. With her help, Garnet would grow strong, the garden would produce lots of potatoes and onions and beans, and the Livingston farm would be a success.

CHAPTER
THREE

A BIG MISTAKE

"It's so nice to have you here," Lydia told Caroline as they walked to the cowshed the next morning. "I've been lonely since we left Sackets Harbor. I—" She stopped suddenly and stared toward the shed.

Caroline felt a flicker of alarm. "What's wrong?"

Lydia pointed to the shed door, which hung slightly open. "I'm sure I latched that last night."

"The cows!" Caroline cried. She flung the door open and ran inside, with Lydia right on her heels. She felt limp with relief when she saw Garnet and Minerva.

Lydia sagged against the wall. "Oh, thank heavens. Maybe I only *thought* I'd latched the door."

25

Or maybe, Caroline thought, *the thief has his eye on Garnet and Minerva.* Perhaps he'd intended to steal the cows, but something had scared him away first.

"I'll tell Papa later," Lydia said. "For now, let's see how our girls are doing."

Caroline and Lydia leaned on the stall railing, watching Garnet nurse hungrily from her mother. Minerva seemed impatient. Every few minutes she walked restlessly away from Garnet.

"See that?" Lydia asked. "Minerva wants Garnet to start eating on her own."

"What will Garnet eat now?" Caroline asked.

"This morning we'll start teaching her to drink milk from a bucket," Lydia said. "We'll gradually change that to water. She'll learn to eat hay and grass and vegetables, too." She fastened a rope halter around Minerva's head. "I'm going to take Minerva outside so Garnet can't nurse. You stand by the door and close it before Garnet can follow us."

Caroline hesitated. "What if Minerva pokes you with her horns?"

"Minerva is as gentle as a lamb," Lydia assured her. "Little Garnet is the one you have to watch out for!"

Lydia led Minerva out to a small pen behind the shed. When Caroline shut the door, Garnet bawled in protest.

Caroline gently patted Garnet. She liked how the calf's thick hair felt both soft and bristly. "Poor thing," Caroline told her. "I know just how you feel. I miss my mother, too."

Garnet turned her head. She seemed to be listening carefully.

"And silly Lydia told me I had to watch out for you," Caroline scoffed. By the time Lydia returned with a bucket of milk, Caroline and Garnet were getting along just fine.

"Time for Garnet's first lesson," Lydia said.

"May I try?" Caroline asked eagerly.

Lydia handed her the bucket. "Dip your fingers in the milk," she instructed.

Caroline put her fingers into the warm milk. "Now what?"

"Put your hand in front of Garnet's mouth and let her suck from your fingers," Lydia said. "Calves don't have upper teeth, so she can't hurt you."

"Want some milk?" Caroline asked, stretching her hand toward Garnet. She held her breath. The calf sniffed once before taking Caroline's fingers into her mouth. Garnet's tongue felt rough, and she sucked with so much force that for a moment Caroline wasn't sure she'd be able to get her fingers back! Once the milk was gone, however, she was able to pull her hand away.

Garnet sucked milk from Caroline's fingers several times. Each time, Caroline held her hand closer and closer to the bucket.

"Now," Lydia said finally, "keep your fingers right at the surface of the milk."

Caroline dipped her fingers back into the milk. Garnet looked at her hand and snorted.

"Come now, Garnet," Caroline coaxed. "You can do it."

Instead of putting her nose into the milk, Garnet butted her head against the bucket—*hard*. Thrown off balance, Caroline stumbled and couldn't stay on her feet. She landed on her backside. A spray of milk landed on her.

Lydia sputtered with laughter. "I told you she was strong!"

Once Caroline was over her surprise, she laughed too. She rose to her feet and dusted herself

*Garnet butted her head against the bucket—**hard**. Caroline stumbled and landed on her backside. Lydia sputtered with laughter.*

off. Bits of straw clung to the back of her skirt, and milk and cow drool streaked the front. "I thought Garnet was ready to drink from the bucket! Why did she hit it?"

"She wasn't being mean," Lydia said. "She butts her head against Minerva when she wants milk. It's her way of saying she's hungry."

The calf gazed up at Caroline with her big, dark eyes as if to say, *I'm sorry you fell down.*

"You're a rascal," Caroline scolded her lightly. "Next time you want something, please be more polite!"

Once the girls had finished tending the cows and cleaning the stall, they tackled the huge vegetable garden. It was surrounded by a board fence so that rabbits and deer couldn't munch the produce. When Lydia opened the gate, it gave a loud screech.

"Gracious!" Caroline clapped her hands over her ears. She hurried inside and waited until Lydia closed the gate behind

them—with another screech—before lowering her
hands again.

"Papa was planning to fix that," Lydia said,
"but now that a thief is about, Papa's glad the gate
screeches. He says we'll hear anyone trying to sneak
into *our* garden."

"I should say so," Caroline agreed.

Lydia looked at the garden and shook her head.
"Mama and I planted lots of seeds, but look how
many weeds have grown in! I can't even tell what
vegetables have sprouted."

"Well," Caroline said briskly, "let's get started."

Caroline had often helped Grandmother in their
garden, so she knew what to do. In the nearest row,
small, lacy carrot plants had poked through the soil in
a tidy line, but tall weeds were choking them. Caroline
knelt and began pulling the weeds carefully, making
sure that she didn't damage any of the carrots. She
wondered if Grandmother was weeding the garden
at home, all by herself. Was she managing?

I'm needed here, Caroline reminded herself. She
took a moment to gently push thoughts of Sackets
Harbor from her mind. Through her skirt, the earth
felt warm against her knees. She heard the ringing

blows of Uncle Aaron's ax as he hacked at a stump in the nearby field, and the contented buzz of a fat bumblebee drifting past, and Lydia's voice when she began to sing a hymn nearby.

Soon the wave of homesickness passed, and Caroline finished weeding her row. "This looks much better," she said, sitting back on her heels and admiring the carrot plants. "Lydia, do you think we should stop for now?" The sun was high overhead.

Lydia wiped sweat from her cheek, leaving a smudge of dirt behind. "Papa will want his midday meal soon," she agreed. She pointed to a far corner of the garden. "There's some asparagus back there that might be ready to eat. Would you look and see? I've gathered some watercress and a few wild leeks this spring, but they don't taste nearly as good as the first bite of fresh asparagus!"

Caroline loved fresh asparagus too—the spring's first tender stalks were a treat after eating wrinkled beets and pickled cabbage all winter. She eagerly made her way to the asparagus patch, making sure not to step on any tiny vegetable plants. The garden's far corner was thick with tall weeds. Caroline pushed them aside, searching. Where was the asparagus? She didn't see any of the straight green spears poking from the earth. Finally she knelt and crawled back and forth, parting weeds with her hands.

Then she stopped short. "Oh no," she moaned. No wonder she'd had trouble finding the asparagus! Every stalk had been sliced off, leaving just the barest nub of green above the soil. "Lydia? Come look at this."

Lydia joined her and stared at the asparagus nubs. "Someone *cut* those."

"I'm afraid so," Caroline said. "And stole every last stalk."

"But how did the thief get into the garden without Papa or me hearing?" Lydia put her hands on her hips, staring at the noisy gate.

Caroline scanned the garden, trying to find an answer. "I suppose someone might have climbed over the fence," she said doubtfully, "but it would have been hard." The boards were tall and smooth.

Lydia stamped one foot. "First the thief took a pail of milk, and now this. I was counting on that asparagus! Just thinking about it made my mouth water." She glared at the damage for a moment. Then she sighed. "I'd better fetch Papa. He'll want to see this."

When Uncle Aaron saw the nubs, he muttered something under his breath.

"And there's more bad news," Caroline told him. "We found the shed door unlatched this morning, too."

Uncle Aaron rubbed his face with one hand. "We can't have any more thievery on our place," he said. "I'll have to start keeping watch at night."

"Oh, Papa," Lydia fretted. "You can't work hard all day and then sit up all night!"

He stared at the asparagus nubs grimly. "If the scoundrel stole vegetables, he might steal Minerva or Garnet next."

Caroline felt a hitch in her chest. Lydia and her father needed those cows. They'd spent the last of their money to buy them! Without those cows, the farm might fail. Besides . . . Caroline couldn't bear the thought of a thief leading those sweet animals away.

"I'll help keep watch," Caroline told her uncle.

"I will as well," Lydia said quickly.

Uncle Aaron put one arm around each girl's shoulders. "You need your sleep, but I will be glad for a bit of help. Don't fear. I'm sure the thief will be caught soon."

Yes, Caroline thought, *but how much more will he steal before that happens?*

That evening, Caroline visited Garnet and Minerva in their pen behind the shed. "There, now," Caroline said soothingly as she approached the calf. "Uncle Aaron said you need to practice being led."

Garnet jumped sideways when Caroline reached for her rope halter. Caroline was glad that the cows were in the small pen, so Garnet didn't have much room to scamper away. Caroline tried again, moving her hand more slowly. This time she grasped the rope. "Good girl!" she said.

Garnet clearly wasn't sure that she wanted to be led, but Caroline managed to tug the calf in a circle around the pen. "You know, Garnet, this would be easier in a bigger space," Caroline said.

A single wooden rail served as a gate between the pen and a fenced pasture. Caroline considered the pasture, which was green and thick with grasses and other plants. "We'd have a lot more room out there."

She slid the rail out of the way and led Garnet through the opening. Minerva followed right behind. Once they were in the pasture, Caroline found it much easier to work with Garnet. Minerva contentedly munched tender green shoots, and Garnet followed Caroline around the pasture with only a few dancing hops of protest.

As they walked, Caroline told Garnet about her own family. Then she described Sackets Harbor. "The lake is bigger and grander than you can imagine," she said. "I love sailing on the lake more than anything else."

Garnet tossed her head.

"Is that enough for now?" Caroline asked. "You've done very well. Let's lead your mama back into the shed, shall we?"

Caroline led Garnet back to the pen and on to the shed. "Come along, Minerva!" Caroline called.

Minerva, happily gobbling grass, ignored her.

This won't do, Caroline thought. She'd never tried to lead Minerva, but Lydia had said the cow was gentle. "I hope that's true," Caroline murmured, eyeing those long, curved horns. Moving very slowly, she approached Minerva and grasped the cow's halter. It took all of Caroline's strength to pull Minerva's head away from her meal. After that, though, the cow seemed willing to be led into the shed.

Caroline was proud of her accomplishment. She'd led both Garnet and Minerva by herself! "Sleep tight," she told the cows as she left them. "I'll help keep watch tonight so that you stay safe." No one was going to steal the Livingston cows if she could help it.

Caroline and Lydia each took a turn sitting up by the front door that night, watching and listening for the thief. There was no sign of trouble, thankfully, but it was a long night. As Caroline made cornmeal mush for breakfast the next morning, she couldn't stop yawning. Uncle Aaron had done most of the guard duty, though, and Caroline knew that he must be even more weary.

"I almost fell asleep while I was milking Minerva," Lydia confessed when she returned from the cowshed with pail in hand. "I put most of the milk in the springhouse to cool, but here's some for our breakfast. And I have a surprise." She proudly pulled three radishes from her pocket. "Fresh from our garden! At least the thief didn't get these."

Uncle Aaron smiled. "Our very first harvest!" He made a show of taking one of the radishes and crunching it between his teeth, closing his eyes while he ate. "I believe," he said, "that this is the finest radish ever grown."

Caroline dished up the cornmeal mush. "Are you going to the Sinclairs' today?" she asked her uncle.

He nodded. "His hay is ready to cut. I'm always happy to help out a neighbor. Mr. Sinclair promised to give me some of the hay in return, too."

Minerva will like that, Caroline thought. She took her place at the table and sleepily poured Uncle Aaron a cup of milk.

When he tasted it, he sputtered and choked and spit the milk back into his cup. "Oh!" he gasped, wiping his mouth with his hand. "That tastes awful!"

Lydia grabbed the milk pitcher and sniffed. "It doesn't smell good, either."

"Minerva must have eaten something she

shouldn't have." Uncle Aaron looked confused. "But how could that be? We've been so careful to keep her in the pen!"

Caroline's cheeks grew hot. *Oh **no**,* she thought.

"I can't imagine," Lydia was saying.

"I can," Caroline said in a small voice. "Yesterday evening, when you were both busy, I . . . I took the cows into the pasture behind their little pen."

Lydia looked dismayed. "That pasture is full of wild leeks! Minerva must have eaten some. That's what spoiled her milk."

"I'm very sorry." Caroline looked from her cousin to her uncle. "I just wanted more room to practice leading Garnet. I didn't know about the leeks!"

Lydia sighed. "I haven't had time to dig them out yet. I should have told you."

Caroline pleated her skirt between her fingers. "How long will Minerva's milk be spoiled?"

"It will taste like onions for several days, probably," Lydia said.

Caroline had often gathered wild leeks in the spring so that Grandmother could cook with them. Caroline liked their oniony taste in soups and stews. But in milk? No.

Then a new thought filled her with panic. "What about Garnet? Will she stop nursing?"

Lydia shook her head. "When she's hungry enough, she'll eat. I'll have to throw the rest of the milk away, though."

Caroline stared at her hands. She'd only wanted to help! Now Lydia wouldn't have milk to churn into butter—butter that she could have sold or traded for something she needed.

"Don't worry, we'll get by," Lydia said. Then she snickered. "And—oh, Papa! I wish you could have seen the look on your face when you tasted that milk!"

"Now, Lydia. Don't be unkind to your father," Uncle Aaron said, chuckling.

Caroline was grateful for their laughter, but she wasn't able to join in. *No more mistakes!* she told herself. On the Livingston farm, every bit of food was too valuable to waste.

ALL ALONE AT THE FARM

After breakfast, Uncle Aaron left to help the Sinclairs. Caroline and Lydia began washing dishes. Caroline tried to think of a way to make up for her mistake. Radishes and cornmeal mush—with no milk—made a poor meal for a farmer.

"Lydia," she asked, "are there any creeks nearby? Perhaps we could catch some fish and surprise your papa with a fine dinner."

Lydia grinned. "Oh, he'd love that," she said. "There's a good stream that's not too far away. I'd better stay here to keep an eye on things, but you could go."

Caroline had hoped that she and Lydia could go

fishing together. That would be much more fun! *But what's most important is helping her and Uncle Aaron,* Caroline reminded herself. "I'll go," she promised. "First, let's get a bit more work done in the garden."

By mid-morning, Caroline had planted melon seeds and cleared the cucumber and onion patches of weeds. Lydia was carefully digging up little cabbage seedlings that had crowded too close together and replanting them where they had more room to grow. As Caroline watched her cousin work, she felt a fresh wave of anger toward the thief. Her cousin, and Uncle Aaron and Aunt Martha too, were working very hard to make this farm a success. How dare someone sneak into the garden and take what didn't belong to him?

A rustle nearby caught Caroline's attention. A chipmunk, its cheeks bulging, darted past and disappeared among some weeds by the fence. "Did you eat my melon seeds?" Caroline demanded. "Those were not for you!" She crawled after him, staying close to the ground. If she could find the chipmunk's hole in the garden fence, she'd try to plug it.

"What are you doing?" Lydia called.

Caroline tugged at a big weed next to the fence. "A chipmunk stole some of the melon seeds! There must be a little tunnel under the fence, or a gap between two boards."

"If you find a hole, fill it in," Lydia said. "I don't want so much as a baby mouse in here."

Caroline searched among the weeds along the fence until she found a knothole near the bottom of one board, big enough to make a nice doorway for mice or chipmunks. She gathered a few stones to block the hole. When she tried to do that, however, she got a surprise. The board moved!

Frowning, Caroline studied it more carefully. The top nail holding this board was still in place, but the bottom nail was missing. Caroline was able to swing the plank back and forth like the pendulum on a mantel clock.

"My goodness!" she said. "Lydia, come and see!"

Lydia patted another cabbage into the dirt before joining Caroline. "I didn't know we had a loose board," she said. "Papa can fix that."

"Do you suppose the thief might have crawled into the garden through this gap?" Caroline asked.

Lydia tipped her head, considering. "It's awfully narrow."

Caroline squinted at the plank. *Could* someone squeeze through that opening? There was one way to find out. She pushed the plank to one side and began wriggling through. "Ooh!" she gasped as the unmoving boards on either side of the opening scraped against her arms. In a moment, though, she was on the far side of the fence.

"If the thief did come through here," she said, "he must be skinny."

"Very skinny indeed." Lydia's voice was still doubtful. "I'm afraid to try it. Wait a moment." Lydia disappeared, and Caroline heard the gate screech open and then screech closed again before her cousin joined her outside the fence.

Lydia frowned, looking from the nearby woods to the loose board. "It wouldn't be hard for a thief to watch from the forest until it was safe to sneak into the garden."

As Caroline considered the gap in the fence, something caught her eye. She pointed to a single red thread snagged on one of the boards beside the loose one. "Look at this!"

Lydia crouched beside her. "I don't own any red clothes," she said. "Papa doesn't either."

"The thread must have come from the thief," Caroline said. "It hasn't been there long enough to fade in the sun. The color is still bright."

"So the thief is very skinny and was wearing something red." Lydia shook her head. "I don't know how that helps us."

"With a better idea of what to look for," Caroline said, "maybe we can find him!"

When Caroline was ready to go fishing, Lydia gave her directions. "Walk to the southwest corner of the field." She pointed. "From there, follow the path downhill through the woods. It will take you to the stream."

"I won't get lost," Caroline assured her.

"If you catch some fish, it will be a wonderful treat for Papa," Lydia said. "It will be fun to surprise him."

As she set out, Caroline realized that she didn't really mind heading to the creek on her own. She'd brought a fishing pole and a moss-lined basket to carry her catch. Stuffed into her pocket was an old tobacco tin holding worms and grasshoppers. Fish could be choosy. She liked having two kinds of bait.

I'll pretend I'm on a treasure hunt, she thought. Catching some fish to surprise Uncle Aaron would be almost as good as finding a gold piece! And with luck, she'd be able to bring back a treat for Lydia, too.

A short way down the trail, Caroline spotted a huge sycamore tree, dead for so long that the trunk was hollow. Had honeybees started a hive inside the trunk? Honey would be a wonderful treat for her cousin. Caroline held her breath and tiptoed closer, watching for bees, listening for the telltale buzzing. The trunk was silent and empty, however.

Caroline returned to the path. Soon she saw some sweet william flowers. *I'll pick those for Lydia on my way back,* she decided. The pretty blossoms would brighten the dark cabin.

Before too long, Caroline reached the stream. The water was clear and fast, tumbling over rocks, gurgling past banks shaded with willows.

This stream must flow to Lake Ontario, she thought with a stab of homesickness. She paused, trying to imagine herself back in Sackets Harbor. What was happening at the shipyard? Was Papa still working on his design for a new sloop? She could almost hear gulls calling and waves slapping at the ship . . .

A woodpecker banged loudly on a nearby tree, startling Caroline from her daydream. "You're here to fish," she reminded herself. "Get busy."

Before trying her luck, she made her way downstream. Sometimes the biggest fish lurked in still pools along the bank. After shoving through the underbrush for a few moments, she spotted just such a pool. "Perfect!" she announced.

Then she saw something else. Someone had stretched a piece of cotton cord over the creek, tying each end to the trunk of a small tree. Several shorter strings had been tied to the cord and dangled into the water. Caroline could see wire hooks dancing just below the surface. None had snagged a fish.

Her pleasure in the fine day vanished as quickly

as a cloud might cross over the sun. Who had left these fishing lines? Was this still Uncle Aaron's land, or was it someone else's property? Caroline wasn't used to worrying about such things. Back home, good fishing spots were so plentiful that anyone could easily find a quiet place to enjoy.

But Caroline wasn't in Sackets Harbor anymore. She didn't know how things were done around here. And she didn't know who was sneaking about at night, stealing from honest folk.

Caroline told herself that the person who had set these fishing lines was most likely a neighbor. And yet, if the thief was an army deserter, hiding in the woods ... well, someone like that might very well try to catch fish in this lonely spot.

Caroline turned in a circle, studying the woods uneasily. She saw no sign of anyone, but she decided not to stay so close to the fishing rig. She followed the stream back to the spot where she'd left the trail.

She still felt nervous. *Perhaps I should go back to the cabin,* she thought. But she'd come here to fish! She forced herself to bait her hook.

By the time shadows stretched long, she'd caught two speckled brook trout. Caroline hesitated. She had hoped to catch more than that! But she couldn't stop wondering if someone might be watching her from behind a nearby tree.

This will do for today, she decided. She dampened the moss in her basket to keep the fish cool. Then she headed for the cabin.

When Caroline got back to the farm, she told Lydia about the fishing rig.

"A neighbor might have left it," Lydia said, "but it's hard to know."

Caroline tried to put her unease out of her mind. "I brought these flowers home for you," she said. Lydia's face glowed when she saw the pretty blossoms.

When Uncle Aaron returned just before dark, dusty and tired, he was delighted to find fried fish, cornbread, and a salad of tart dandelion greens waiting. "What a feast!" he exclaimed. "Thank you, girls."

Caroline felt warm inside. She'd come to help with chores, but it felt even better to cheer up her cousin and uncle.

"I thought we might share one fish tonight and save the other for tomorrow," Lydia told her father. "I put it in the springhouse to keep it from spoiling."

"Uncle Aaron, someone left a fishing line strung over the creek," Caroline said. "Do you think it might have been left by the thief?"

Uncle Aaron frowned slightly. "Perhaps. I don't recall ever seeing a rig like that around here."

For a moment, no one spoke. Caroline imagined a runaway soldier creeping through the woods near the farm. The picture made her shiver.

"Will you need to help at the Sinclair place tomorrow?" Lydia asked her father.

"The job's not finished, so I will," Uncle Aaron replied. He forked up another small bite of trout, clearly savoring every morsel. "Mrs. Sinclair reminded me about her Independence Day picnic," he added. "It will be a fun day."

But not as fun as Independence Day in Sackets Harbor, Caroline thought wistfully.

"Lydia, Mrs. Sinclair asked if you'd be willing to come with me tomorrow," Uncle Aaron said. "She has half a dozen men to feed at midday, and she'd be glad of your help."

Caroline stopped eating. "What about me?" she asked.

"I wish we could take you as well," Uncle Aaron began, "but..."

"But someone must stay and watch for the thief," Caroline said. She swallowed hard. She didn't like the idea of being alone all day, but she tried not to show it. "I understand."

Uncle Aaron seemed to guess her feelings. "The thief has always struck at night," he reminded her. "There's no reason to think he would try to steal something in daylight."

Lydia clapped a hand over her mouth. "Oh! That reminds me. Caroline discovered something else today." She described the loose board and showed her father the red thread.

"I'll nail the loose board down right away," he said. He finished the water in his mug, wiped his mouth on his sleeve, and got to his feet. "If the scoundrel used that gap to slip into our garden, he'll be surprised if he comes back."

That night, when Caroline took her turn keeping watch by the front door, she reminded herself that the thief would have to use the screechy gate to reach the garden now. She sat on the front step in the darkness, feeling very alone, straining her eyes and her ears for any hint of an intruder. An owl hooted once, but that was all.

Maybe the thief has moved on, she thought. Since she'd be all alone on the farm the next day, she wanted to believe that he'd done just that.

Caroline waved good-bye to Uncle Aaron and Lydia when they set off for the Sinclair farm. Uncle Aaron carried a hay fork over one shoulder. "We'll be home as soon as we can," he promised.

"Don't worry," Caroline said stoutly. "I'll be fine." Still, once they'd disappeared down the lane, she felt lonely.

But I'm not truly alone, Caroline reminded herself. She still had Minerva and Garnet for company.

Lydia had left the cows in their shed. Caroline decided to visit them before washing the breakfast dishes. She felt better when Minerva turned her head and gave a low *moo-oo* of greeting. Caroline liked her warm cow smell, and the way Garnet peeked out from beneath her long, dark lashes as if she were too shy to say good morning.

"Garnet," Caroline said, "may I lead you around your pen a few times? It will be good practice."

Garnet gave a little sideways prance.

Caroline laughed. "That must mean you're ready to go." She was able to grab the calf's halter easily this time. "Good girl," she crooned as she led Garnet to the door.

Caroline was about to step outside when a sudden spot of color caught her eye. Something red flashed in the trees on the far side of the clearing. Caroline stood still as stone, peeping around the door frame. There it was again! Something was moving through the underbrush—something as red as a cardinal, but bigger.

Was it someone wearing a shirt as red as the thread she'd found on the garden fence?

Caroline jumped back into the dim shed, heart pounding. Uncle Aaron was gone. Lydia was gone. Had the thief watched them leave? Was he prowling around the farm believing that no one was home?

What should I do? Caroline thought desperately. Her first impulse was to run into the cabin, latch the door, and stay there until Uncle Aaron and Lydia got home.

Garnet bumped her nose against Caroline's hip. She seemed to be saying, *What about me?* Caroline swallowed. She couldn't simply hide in the cabin and leave the garden and the cows to the thief.

I could hide the cows in the woods, Caroline thought. If she did that, the garden would be left unprotected. But if she stood watch in the garden and left Minerva and Garnet here, the thief might steal them both!

Whatever she did, Caroline knew she had to act fast. *It would be easier for Uncle Aaron and Lydia to get new vegetable seeds,* she decided, *than a new cow and calf.*

Caroline held her breath and peeked outside, scanning the cabin, the yard, the garden fence, the woods. Everything seemed still. She waited. Had she imagined the intruder? No! She caught her breath as someone wearing a red shirt slipped from the trees. He appeared to be a young man, skinny and perhaps not yet full-grown. Crouched over, he darted toward the garden and disappeared behind the tall fence.

Caroline knew she didn't have much time. When the thief discovered that the loose board had been nailed down, he might reappear in the yard.

Plucking up her courage, she turned to the cows. "You're coming with me," she whispered. "Garnet, I'm going to lead you into the woods. Minerva, I expect you to follow. *Hurry!*"

Garnet came along without fuss. *Thank goodness we practiced,* Caroline thought. To her relief, Minerva ambled along behind, unwilling to be separated from her calf.

Caroline led the cows out the shed door and around the corner so that the small building hid them from sight. From there, she tugged Garnet into the woods. Minerva followed, but as soon as they left the bare-earth farmyard, the cow lowered her head and began tearing at grasses with her teeth.

"No, stop!" Caroline hissed. She grabbed Minerva's halter with her free hand and tugged frantically until she managed to pull the cow's head up. With every step, Minerva tried again to snatch some fresh greens. Caroline struggled to keep her moving until they were screened behind a dense thicket. Then she gave up and rested her aching arms, letting the cow have her way.

A distant *screeech* echoed through the quiet morning. The thief had opened the garden gate!

He must believe the farm was deserted. And once he'd raided the garden, he might come to steal the cows.

I need to find a better hiding place for Minerva and Garnet, Caroline thought. *But where?*

The sound of munching caught her attention. Minerva was happily eating a thick clump of plants that Caroline didn't recognize. Her heart sank. On top of everything else, the cow's milk might be ruined again...

Wait! Thinking of milk gave Caroline a new idea. *Maybe I can hide Minerva and Garnet in the springhouse,* she thought, feeling a flicker of hope. The springhouse was close by, but it was so overgrown with briars and vines that the thief likely didn't know it existed.

Caroline tugged Minerva's halter. The cow raised her head with a disapproving look. "I'm sorry," Caroline whispered, "but this is for your own good." Creeping through the underbrush as quietly as possible, she led Minerva and Garnet to the springhouse. She managed to unbolt the door with one hand.

Minerva eyed the door and tossed her head with alarm. *Oh no,* Caroline moaned silently. If Minerva started bellowing, the thief would surely hear.

"Please, Minerva, be good!" Caroline begged in a hoarse whisper as she pulled the cow's halter again. "I'm trying to save you and your baby."

Minerva stayed quiet but tossed her head again and didn't move. Seconds ticked past. Finally Caroline let go of her halter and looked at Garnet. "Show your mama," Caroline whispered. She led Garnet, step by step, into the springhouse. Minerva hesitated, but she followed her calf. Caroline quickly shut the door behind them.

Minerva swung her head from side to side and stamped one foot. Caroline was still afraid that the cow might make a racket.

Then, as if knowing that Caroline needed help, Garnet bumped her head against Minerva to say, *I'm hungry!* The calf began to nurse. And Minerva settled down.

"Good girls," Caroline told them. "I'll be back for you as soon as I can!"

CHAPTER
FIVE

INDEPENDENCE DAY

 Once the cows were settled, Caroline slipped from the springhouse and latched the door behind her. For a moment she felt a sense of triumph. She'd hidden the cows!

But where was the thief? Was he still stuffing his pockets in the garden? Caroline didn't dare confront him. *But I should try to get a better look at him,* she thought. If she could describe the thief, Uncle Aaron might be able to catch him.

Caroline crept to the cowshed, slipped inside, and grabbed a pitchfork from among the tools hanging on one wall. She couldn't imagine using it to defend herself, but holding it made her feel braver.

Then she peeked around the door frame. Across the yard, the garden gate stood wide open. She held her breath. Had the thief already dug all the radishes and tiny carrots and slipped back into the woods? Maybe he'd decided to raid the cabin, too. But no—as she watched, the intruder walked out through the garden gate. He wore a brown hat pulled low, and dark trousers with his red shirt.

Caroline jerked backward so that he wouldn't see her—and the pitchfork banged into a sickle hanging on the wall. It fell to the ground, clattering against a tin pail. It sounded as loud as thunder. Caroline's heart jumped to her throat as the thief froze, staring straight at her. Then he began to run.

If he'd come toward her, Caroline would have turned and raced all the way to Sackets Harbor! Instead, the thief was running away. And without giving it any thought, Caroline tightened her grip on the pitchfork and ran after him.

The thief pounded along the edge of Uncle Aaron's field. Although he had a head start, Caroline managed to gain on him. He was barefoot. Several times he seemed to step on a stone or stick and took several hops on one foot before running on.

Caroline raced after him. Her fear slid away, replaced with anger. She would scare this thief so that he'd never want to steal again!

At the back corner of the field, he turned down the path that led to the stream. Caroline had nearly caught up to him when she caught one foot on a root. She stumbled and almost fell. When she looked up again, the path ahead was empty.

Where could the thief have gone? Caroline stopped, gasping for breath, searching the underbrush for any telltale movement or flash of red cloth. Everything was still and silent. *He must be here somewhere!* she thought, bewildered.

Then she remembered the dead sycamore—the one with the hollow trunk. Holding the pitchfork firmly in both hands, she crept toward the tree. The opening faced away from her, but as she got close, she saw a pair of dirty feet poking from the hidey-hole.

She tiptoed closer, circling around the trunk. The thief was crammed inside the tree, sitting with his knees pulled up against his chest. He was younger than she'd expected—maybe twelve or fourteen. Was he a young boy from the navy who'd run away from his ship?

Caroline's fear slid away, replaced with anger.
She would scare this thief so that he'd never want to steal again!

"Come out of there!" Caroline demanded.

After a moment, the boy crept into the open. "Don't hurt me," he begged, eyeing the pitchfork. "Please don't poke me with that!"

He looked so frightened that Caroline lowered the pitchfork. She was still angry, though. "You have no right to be sneaking about, stealing things that don't belong to you!"

The boy shoved his hands into his pockets, hunched his shoulders, and stared at his toes. "I didn't think anyone was home," he mumbled.

"That doesn't make it right!" Caroline glared at him. "Well? Why have you been stealing?"

The boy was quiet for a long moment. Then his knees seemed to buckle, and he folded to the ground. He buried his face in his hands, but not before Caroline saw tears welling in his eyes. "I'm just so *hungry*," he whispered.

Caroline's anger drained away. For the first time, she noticed how thin the boy was, and how ragged and dirty his clothes were. "What's your name?" she asked gently.

"R-Robbie," he managed, swiping at his eyes. "Robbie Parkhurst."

Caroline chewed her lower lip, wishing Uncle Aaron and Lydia were here. They weren't, though. It was up to her to handle this situation.

"Come along, Robbie," she said. She grabbed his hand and pulled him to his feet. "Let's go find you some food."

A short while later Caroline sat at the table in the cabin, watching Robbie wolf the cornmeal mush and fried fish she'd put in front of him. When he was finished, he wiped the plate with his fingers and licked them clean. "Thank you," he said. "I surely appreciate your kindness. I'll be going now." He started to rise.

"No, wait!" Caroline protested. "Please."

Robbie reluctantly dropped back down on the bench.

"Why are you so hungry?" Caroline asked. "Don't you have any parents?"

"My father was a soldier," Robbie said quietly. "He was killed in the battle at Sackets Harbor."

The grief in his eyes made Caroline's heart ache.

"I'm sorry," she said. "My papa fought in that battle, and I know it was horrible. What about your mother?"

"My mama always followed the army," Robbie told her. "Me and my two little sisters, too. Mama did laundry for the men in my father's regiment, and my sisters and I did chores. In return, the army gave us blankets and a little food. But now . . ." He spread his hands, palms up. "Once Pa got killed, we had to leave the regiment."

Caroline frowned. "Why? Couldn't your mother keep washing clothes for the soldiers?"

"Army regulations say that once a woman gets widowed, she either has to marry another soldier or move on," Robbie explained. "Mama's not ready to marry again—she's brokenhearted about Pa. We've got no family anywhere near, so we just set out down the road."

Caroline couldn't imagine simply wandering, with nowhere to go. "What happened?"

Robbie shrugged sadly. "My mama hasn't been able to think straight. She's been sickly, too. When we came to an abandoned farm near here, I decided we should hole up until she got stronger and we could figure out what to do next. The cabin roof has fallen

64

in, but there's an animal shed yet standing. We've been sleeping there. I've tried to keep us fed with wild greens and frogs and such, but I can't always find enough."

Caroline looked away. What a terrible situation!

"Please don't tell anyone," Robbie begged. "Pa would be ashamed if he could see us now."

"Were you the one who set that fishing line across the creek?" Caroline asked.

Robbie nodded. "I've never fished before, though, and I must have baited the hooks wrong. Every one was empty when I got back." He rubbed a rough spot on the table with his thumb. "It got so my sisters couldn't sleep at night. They were so hungry, they just cried. That's when I started stealing. I know it's wrong, but..." His voice faded away.

Caroline got up and walked to the window, trying to think. She understood that Robbie was truly desperate. Stealing *was* wrong ... and yet if someone in her family wept from hunger, she might do the same thing.

"I'm feeling better after this fine meal," Robbie said. "I'll just go and collect my family, and we'll set off for someplace new. No one needs to know."

Caroline faced him. "I can't keep this a secret from my Uncle Aaron and cousin Lydia. This is their farm, and you've eaten some of their food."

Robbie hung his head.

"But I'm sure they'll understand," Caroline added. She looked around the cabin. There was precious little food inside, and not much yet ripe in the garden. And she'd come here to help her relatives, not give their food away! *But Uncle Aaron trusted me enough to leave me alone today,* she thought. *I have to make the best choice I can.* And with that, she knew exactly what to do.

"We don't have much food to spare," Caroline told Robbie, "but let me see what I can find, and we'll take it to your family."

He stared at her with wide eyes. "Honest?"

"Shall we take some milk for your sisters?" she asked. "But—oh." She made a face. "It will taste like leeks."

"That's of no matter at all," Robbie assured her. He jumped to his feet, looking downright hopeful. "They'll be ever so pleased."

Caroline walked to the abandoned farm with Robbie. The small clearing was silent. Robbie led her to the rickety shed. Inside, two little girls with dirty faces and big eyes sat huddled in one corner.  Mrs. Parkhurst, who looked completely done in with grief and hunger, lay on a blanket. A canvas sack hung on the wall. *That sack,* Caroline thought, *must hold everything the Parkhursts have left in the world.*

The girls scooted away when they saw Caroline follow Robbie inside. Mrs. Parkhurst tried to sit up. She looked alarmed.

"Please, don't worry," Caroline told them gently. "Robbie and I brought a little food."

Robbie set down a crock of cornmeal mush. Caroline carefully poured milk from another crock into a tin cup. She offered it to Mrs. Parkhurst, who waved a hand toward her daughters. "If you'd be so kind," she said, "please feed my girls first."

The girls drank greedily. They didn't seem to mind the flavor of wild leeks.

We considered that milk ruined, Caroline thought. She'd been worried about Lydia and Uncle Aaron

Caroline poured milk into a tin cup. "If you'd be so kind,"
Mrs. Parkhurst said, "please feed my girls first."

having enough food. Compared to the Parkhursts, though, the Livingston family was eating very well indeed.

Caroline noticed Mrs. Parkhurst smoothing her hair as if she was uncomfortable to have a stranger see her in such a sad state. "I need to go now," Caroline told them, "but I'll be back later. I promise."

When Uncle Aaron and Lydia returned home that afternoon, Caroline told them everything that had happened. "I'm sorry I gave away food without your permission," she said. "I just couldn't bear to see anyone so hungry."

Uncle Aaron put his hands on her shoulders— just as Papa might have done when he had something important to tell her. "You did just fine today, Caroline. First you protected the cows. Then you helped a family that is truly in need. I'm proud of you."

Caroline felt a warm glow spread inside. "Thank you, Uncle Aaron."

He cocked his head toward the door. "Now, let's

go fetch the Parkhursts. They can sleep snug under
our roof tonight."

By the time the Parkhursts were settled into the
loft in the Livingstons' cabin, darkness had cloaked
the farm. Lydia and Caroline lit a lantern and walked
to the cowshed to check on Minerva and Garnet.
"I felt awful about spoiling Minerva's milk, but you
should have seen how Robbie's sisters drank it down,"
Caroline said slowly. "Even though my family's been
living in the middle of war in Sackets Harbor, we
never had to worry about where our next meal was
coming from, or where to live."

"I'll never feel sorry for myself for not having
sugar again," Lydia declared. She picked up two
curry brushes and handed one to Caroline.

The girls spent some time brushing the cows.
Garnet pranced about for only a moment before she
quieted down and let Caroline smooth her red coat.
"Good girl," Caroline whispered. "Thank you for
helping me today."

When she and Lydia started back to the cabin,

Caroline paused to admire the stars twinkling overhead. These were the same stars she'd seen from her own home. The same stars that sailors used to help guide their ships on the great waters of Lake Ontario. Those stars reminded Caroline that she was still connected to her family, and to Sackets Harbor.

Caroline had long dreamed of sailing her own ship, letting the winds and stars help steer her course. That longing would always fill her heart. *But I will try hard not to feel homesick here, or to feel sorry for myself because I don't have a ship,* she promised herself. For someone like Robbie, her dreams would seem like luxuries indeed.

The cabin door opened. In the shadows, Caroline saw Uncle Aaron step outside and stroll across the yard to join them. "I've just had a good talk with Robbie and his mother," he told Caroline and Lydia. "I've convinced them to stay with us for a few days to gather their strength. In return, they'll help us with chores. Mrs. Parkhurst seems like a sensible woman. Once she's had a few good meals and a chance to rest, she'll be able to decide what she wants to do next."

Caroline and Lydia exchanged delighted smiles. "That's a wonderful plan!" Lydia said.

Uncle Aaron turned to Caroline. "With Mrs. Parkhurst here to help us, we can spare you for a few days. Would you like to celebrate Independence Day in Sackets Harbor?"

Caroline gasped, then threw her arms around her uncle. "Oh, *yes*! I'll come back and help here afterward, but—oh, I did *so* want to be home on Independence Day."

Uncle Aaron laughed. "And so you shall be." Then he tipped his head back and looked at the stars. "It's a fine night."

"It is," Caroline said happily. "It is indeed."

Independence Day in Sackets Harbor was everything that Caroline had hoped it would be. Townspeople and military men gathered by the harbor. Several of the officers gave rousing speeches. Caroline swelled with pride as they spoke of defending their young country.

Then every ship in the harbor fired a gun salute in honor of American independence.

72

Boom! Boom! Boom! The noise shuddered over the water. Caroline gazed north, toward the British troops in Upper Canada that had twice attacked her village. *We are still Americans,* she told them silently. *We will continue to fight until you let us be!*

When the official ceremony was over, the Abbott family and their workers and friends shared a picnic at the shipyard. The men set up big tables, and the ladies set out bowls and baskets of food. The sun was hot, but a breeze ruffled the American flag flying over Abbott's. Caroline smiled as she watched these people she loved enjoy the afternoon.

She was finishing a bowl of wild strawberries served in cream—sweet cream, that didn't taste like leeks—when she heard Papa calling her.

"Yes, Papa?" Caroline put her bowl aside and hurried to join him.

"Will you walk with me?"

"Of course!" She studied his face anxiously, wondering if he had bad news to tell her, but Papa's face was calm. She took his hand.

"Close your eyes," he instructed. The corners of his mouth crinkled, as if he was trying to hide a smile. "I'll guide you."

Where was Papa taking her? Caroline felt an excited tingle as she closed her eyes and let him lead her away. After a moment she heard the hollow sound of wood beneath her shoes. Papa had brought her onto the dock.

"You can look now," Papa said.

Caroline opened her eyes and saw a sweet little skiff sailing into the harbor, heading toward the shipyard. The sight sparked a bittersweet memory. "It looks like *Sparrow*," she said.

Papa's eyes were merry. "It *is*."

"*What?*" Caroline squinted toward the skiff. It did look just like *Sparrow*. Mr. Tate, the chief carpenter, was sailing the skiff. As it drew closer, he dropped the sail so that he could row to the dock.

Caroline turned to her father with astonishment. "But—but I sank *Sparrow* in Hickory Creek weeks ago! I *ruined* her!"

"Not quite ruined," her father said. "Ever since you told me what happened, I've wanted to raise the skiff so I could see if the damage could be repaired. I knew it would please you."

A lump rose in Caroline's throat. With all that Papa had to worry about, all he had to do, he'd thought about raising the skiff? To please *her*?

"That morning when Aaron's letter arrived," Papa continued, "I *knew* you didn't want to leave home. Yet you went without complaint. It helped me realize how much you've grown up since the war began."

Caroline opened her mouth, then closed it again. She couldn't find words.

"So Mr. Tate and I salvaged the skiff. As it turned out, the damage was easy to repair." Papa's voice was full of mischief. "And once the woodwork was sound, I decided the skiff needed a new name." He pointed.

The skiff had almost reached the dock. Grinning, Mr. Tate used the oars to turn the boat broadside. Caroline gasped when she saw the new name spelled out in fresh blue paint: *Miss Caroline*.

"Would you like to go for a sail?" Papa asked.

Caroline clapped her hands. "Oh, *yes!*"

Soon she and Papa were settled into the skiff. Their friends and family waved from the dock. As Papa rowed through the harbor, a military band on shore struck up a tune. The crisp rattle of drums and the clear tones of bugles drifted over the water. It was fine music for Independence Day, both fierce and lively.

The skiff sailed out of the harbor and into the open water of Lake Ontario. Waves danced blue and green into the distance. Caroline laughed for the pure joy of it all. "Shall I raise the sail?" she asked.

"You're the captain," Papa told her.

Within minutes, Caroline had set the sail. *Snap!* The wind caught the canvas. *Miss Caroline* skimmed over the water. A gull called as it glided overhead.

Caroline felt her spirits rise even higher, and soar toward the horizon.

LOOKING BACK

CHANGES FOR AMERICA
IN
1812

American and British diplomats agree to end the war.
The paper at right shows their names signed on the treaty.

Almost as soon as the War of 1812 started, the governments of the United States and Britain wanted to find a way to end it. Finally, in the summer of 1814, leaders from the two countries met in Ghent, a city in Europe, to try to talk out their differences. On the day before Christmas 1814, they signed a *treaty*, or agreement, to end the war.

The Treaty of Ghent didn't stop the fighting—at least not right away. News traveled slowly by ship across the Atlantic Ocean, so word of the agreement didn't reach America for nearly two months. In the meantime, unaware that their leaders had agreed to end the war, British and American soldiers fought one more big battle. On January 8, 1815, the British Army invaded New Orleans. American soldiers fought them so fiercely that in only two hours the British gave up and retreated.

In the war's last battle, American troops fought back a huge British force at New Orleans.

Jubilant Americans celebrate news of the war's end in 1815.

About a month later, the ship carrying news of the treaty arrived at a harbor near New York City. As the news traveled across the nation, Americans like Caroline's family were overjoyed to learn that the war was finally over. They celebrated by shooting fireworks, ringing bells, and holding parades. At last, life could go back to normal!

Because American soldiers had beaten the British at New Orleans, many Americans felt their country had won the war. But some experts say that the War of 1812 was a war that "nobody won." The conflict brought great suffering to both sides. About 2,000 soldiers and sailors were killed on each side, and thousands more were wounded in battle. In addition, great numbers of civilians, like Robbie Parkhurst and his family in the story, suffered or died because the war kept them from getting medical care or enough to eat. And in the end, after almost three years of fighting, the treaty required both countries to give back the territories they'd taken from each other during the war. Neither side gained or lost even an inch of land.

Still, some important things did change. Because

A factory in the 1820s

shipping was blocked during the war, the United States could not get goods from other countries, so American businesses started making more products. After the war, manufacturing continued to grow quickly, bringing great wealth to the country.

In addition, by winning several key battles against the British—the strongest fighting force in the world—the young United States proved to other countries that it was a nation on the rise and its independence had to be respected. The war also gave Americans their national anthem, created a new reverence for the flag, and established a sense of national pride.

Britain and Canada would never fight America again. In fact, both countries

This painting shows the American warship Constitution *winning a famous battle at sea.*

would become firm friends and allies of the United States. The war gave Canadians a new sense of pride and identity, too. The United States stopped trying to expand its borders north into Canada. Instead, American settlers focused on pushing west.

A family heading west

New England had become crowded, and young people were finding it harder and harder to start farms or businesses there. In search of open land and new opportunities, some moved to western New York. Others ventured even farther, to the new and fast-growing state of Ohio. So many new towns were springing up in Ohio, people joked that they were running out of names for them. In the years after the war, settlers pushed into the territories of Indiana, Michigan, and Illinois and still farther west into the vast lands beyond the Mississippi River.

It could take years to build a farm out of the forest. Families often began much the way that Caroline's Uncle Aaron, Aunt Martha, and cousin Lydia did. First, they cleared a small patch of land, either by chopping down trees or by cutting away rings of bark around the

Clearing a field out of the forest

trunks so that the trees would wither and die. Bushes and shrubs were burned away, filling the sky with smoke for months at a time. Amid the rocks, stumps, and roots that could not easily be removed, the family planted its first crops. Gradually, a farmer cleared more land, making room for a barn, livestock, and more crops.

This log cabin is typical of ones built in New York in Caroline's time. You can see it today at Genesee Country Village and Museum in Mumford, New York.

Like Lydia's family, settlers usually started out living in a cramped, rough cabin with a dirt floor. The roof and walls were often full of cracks. There were many ways for rain, cold air, and even small animals to sneak in. Girls like Lydia got used to sharing their homes with insects, mice, and other pests! As soon as they could afford to, a frontier family improved their cabin or built a new, more comfortable farmhouse.

Life on a new farm meant hard work for everyone in the family. As soon as he or she was able, the youngest child might be responsible for hauling drinking water from streams, clearing stones from fields, and gathering firewood. Older children like Lydia had even more to do.

Louisa Collins, a girl living on a farm in 1815, kept a record of chores in her diary. She milked cows, raked hay, picked currants and bayberries, made wine, churned butter, spun wool to make yarn, and sewed clothes. And that was all in just one week! "I shall retire early tonight," she wrote one night, "for I feel quite tired after my day's work."

In such isolated and challenging circumstances, people often became especially close to their family and friends. Neighbors grew to trust and rely on one another, just as Uncle Aaron and the Sinclairs do.

The prospect of backbreaking work and rough living conditions didn't stop settlers from flocking to the frontier. In the four years after the war ended, America gained four new states to the south and west: Indiana, Mississippi, Illinois, and Alabama.

The swift flow of people to the new frontier changed the nation. Settlers cleared forests and plowed up prairies, established farms, and built towns and roads, altering

Settlers in western New York built farms and towns along the Erie Canal, a man-made waterway finished in 1825.

the landscape dramatically. Native American ways of life in these regions were also changed forever.

America's push westward would one day allow it to become one of the largest and most diverse countries in the world. Eventually, America would stretch all the way from the Atlantic Ocean in the east to the Pacific Ocean in the west—"from sea to shining sea." The promise of land and opportunity brought people to the frontier from all over the world. Just like Caroline's and Lydia's families, the newcomers hoped to build houses, farms, and businesses through persistence and hard work. America was fast becoming a place that people of nearly every background and heritage could call home.

READ ALL OF CAROLINE'S STORIES,
available at bookstores and *americangirl.com.*

MEET CAROLINE
When the British attack Caroline's village, she
makes a daring choice that helps to win the day.

CAROLINE'S SECRET MESSAGE
Caroline and Mama take a dangerous journey
to the British fort where Papa is held prisoner.

A SURPRISE FOR CAROLINE
Caroline finds herself on thin ice after
friendship troubles lead to a bad decision!

CAROLINE TAKES A CHANCE
When a warship threatens American supplies,
can Caroline's little fishing boat turn it away?

CAROLINE'S BATTLE
As a battle rages right in her own village,
Caroline faces a terrible choice.

CHANGES FOR CAROLINE
Caroline pitches in on her cousin's new farm—
and comes home to a wonderful surprise.